Library of Congress Cataloging in Publication Data:
Elliott, Dan. Oscar's rotten birthday. (Sesame Street start-to-read books) "Children's Television
Workshop." SUMMARY: Everyone on Sesame Street helps Oscar to have the rottenest birthday ever.
[1. Birthdays—Fiction] I. Henson, Jim. II. Chartier, Normand [date]. III. Children's Television
Workshop. IV. Sesame Street. V. Title. VI. Series. PZ7.E4350s [Fic] AACR2 81-2398
ISBN: 0-394-84848-9 (trade); 0-394-94848-3 (lib. bdg.) Manufactured in the United States of America
9 0

A Sesame Street Start-to-Read Book™

Oscar's Rotten Birthday

by Dan Elliott

illustrated by Normand Chartier

Featuring Jim Henson's Sesame Street Muppets

Random House/Children's Television Workshop

Oscar the Grouch
lives in a trash can
on Sesame Street.

Every day the Mudman brings
Oscar a jar of mud.
Oscar loves mud.
He also loves rotten eggs
and broken toys.

Oscar hates pretty flowers.
He also hates ice cream
and furry kittens.

One day Oscar heard
Ernie and Bert talking.
"This will be the best
birthday party ever,"
Ernie said.

"Yucch! Who is having
a party?" asked Oscar.
Ernie and Bert smiled.
"We can't tell you," they said.
"It's a surprise."

"Who cares?" yelled Oscar.
"I hate birthday parties!"
Ernie and Bert walked away.
Then Oscar remembered.
"Oh, no!" he growled.
"Today is MY birthday!"

"I hate parties!" he shouted.
"I hate party games and
presents and birthday songs!"
But Ernie and Bert were gone.
No one heard Oscar.

Everyone on Sesame Street
was getting ready
for Oscar's birthday party.

Cookie Monster made a cake
all by himself.
Now he needed a big cake box.
The baker on Sesame Street
was happy to help him.

Grover was busy in the woods.
He was looking for a present
for Oscar.

"Oh, Oscar will be so happy!"
said Grover.

Big Bird was busy, too.
He was writing
a birthday song for Oscar.

"Songs are not easy to write . . .
even for us birds,"
said Big Bird.

Everyone on Sesame Street was busy.

Busy finding presents.

Busy making presents.

Busy wrapping presents.

At last it was time
for the party to start.
Everyone was ready.

Oscar was ready, too.
He put a sign on his can.
It said: GO AWAY!

He put on dark glasses.

"When they come," he said,

"I won't see them!"

He put on earmuffs.

"When they sing," he said,

"I won't hear them!"

Then he slammed down his lid.

MMM ...YUM, YUM.. GOOD SONG!

Everyone came to the party.
Cookie came with his cake.
Grover came with his present.
Everyone brought something.

Big Bird gave everyone
a piece of paper.
"Here are the words to
my new song!" he said.

Then they all sang.
"Rotten birthday to you,
rotten birthday to you,
rotten birthday, grouchy Oscar,
rotten birthday to you!"

Oscar popped up in his can.
"Hey! That's a great song!"
he said.

Grover gave Oscar his present.
"I picked them myself," said Grover.
Oscar said, "Yucch! Flowers!"
Then he tore off
the wrapping paper.

Oscar smiled.

"It's stinkweed!" he said.

"Nice, smelly stinkweed!

Hey! Thanks, Grover."

Ernie and Bert gave Oscar
two broken toys.
Betty Lou gave him
a bag of peanut shells.

There were other presents, too.
There was an old sock,
a flat tire,
a jar of mud,
and a broken clock.

Then everyone played games.
They played
Pin the Tail on the Pig,
Toss the Trash in the Can,
and Dunk for Rotten Apples.

When they finished playing,
Cookie said, "Time for cake!"
He gave Oscar the big box.
"Ugh," Oscar said.
"I hate birthday cakes!"

Oscar opened the box.
There was a big cake inside.
A dirty, messy mud cake
with one broken candle.

"Wow! That's a great cake!"
said Oscar.
"Thanks, Cookie Monster."

"This is the best—
I mean the worst—
birthday party ever!"
said Oscar.
Then he frowned.

"Hey! I just thought of something awful,"
he said. "Now I have to wait
a whole year until my next
rotten birthday!"
He slammed down his lid.
And everyone sang
"Rotten birthday, grouchy Oscar"
one more time.